WHAT DO YOU WANT TO BE, BRIAN?

For my wee boy, Ruaraidh - M.R.

For Adam, Alicia and Danny - J.W.

WHAT DO YOU WANT TO BE, BRIAN?

Written by Jeanne Willis

Illustrated by Mary Rees

Andersen Press • London

Text copyright © 1996 by Jeanne Willis. Illustration copyright © 1996 by Mary Rees.
This special paperback edition first published in 2003 by Andersen Press Ltd.
The rights of Jeanne Willis and Mary Rees to be identified as the author and illustrator
of this work have been asserted by them in accordance with the Copyright, Designs and Patents Act, 1988.
First published in Great Britain in 1996 by Andersen Press Ltd. 20 Vauxhall Bridge Road, London SW1V 2SA.
Published in Australia by Random House Australia Pty., 20 Alfred Street, Milsons Point, Sydney, NSW 2061.
All rights reserved. Colour separated in Switzerland by Photolitho AG, Zürich.
Printed and bound in China.

10 9 8 7 6 5 4 3 2 1

British Library Cataloguing in Publication Data available.

ISBN 1 84270 263 7

This book has been printed on acid-free paper

What do you want to be, Brian?

"He wants to be the greatest violinist since Yehudi
Menuhin," said his mother.
"Do I?" said Brian.

"You do," said his mother and she bought him a violin and
made him practise for two hours every day.

Brian tried, but the strings kept snapping and he would keep sticking his bow where he shouldn't.

"He doesn't want to be a violinist," said his father, "he wants to be a computer wizard, like me, don't you, son?"

"Well…" said Brian.

"Of course you do!" said his father. "I've spent an absolute
mint on this new computer."

Brian did his best, but the instructions went in one ear and straight out of the other. Then the wretched thing blew up.

"He doesn't want to be a computer wizard," said his sister,
"he wants to be the most famous ballet dancer since Nureyev."

"I…" said Brian.
"Shut up and put these tights on," said his sister.

Brian really tried, but he kept dropping the ballerinas.
And he accidentally kicked the pianist off her stool. And
he snagged his tights.

"I'm telling you, he wants to be a boxer," said Brian's brother. "He wants to be the heavyweight champion of the world. Come on, Brian, put your mitts up."

But Brian preferred his nose the way it was.

"That lad wants to be the best jockey since Lester Piggott," said his uncle. "You want to get him a horse."

"I wouldn't bet on it," said Brian.

"Horse?" snorted his auntie. "What good is a horse when it's quite plain to me he wants to be an artist, like Van Gogh."

"He wants to be an admiral," said the vet, "like Nelson."

"He wants to be a politician!" said the man who sells
funny little brushes door to door.

"STOP!" shouted Brian. "I want to be…

"…I want to be…"

"Well, what DO you want to be, Brian?"

"I want to be the most ordinary little boy in the world,"
said Brian. And guess what …

… he was brilliant at it.